The Haunting of Merci Hospital

Some Patients Never Leave...

Tanya R. Taylor

This one's for you, "The Dealer".

I hope you enjoy this book and that we never end up like some of those in this story who have lost their way – and were never able to find it again. (*wink*)

Find the yellow door!

OTHER FICTION TITLES BY THIS AUTHOR

INFESTATION: A Small Town Nightmare (The Complete Series)

Real Illusions: The Awakening

Real Illusions II: REBIRTH

Real Illusions III: BONE OF MY BONE

Real Illusions IV: WAR ZONE

Cornelius (Book 1 in the Cornelius saga.)

Revenge of Cornelius (Book 2 in the Cornelius saga.

Each book in this series is a stand-alone.)

CARA: Some Children Keep Terrible Secrets (Book 3 in the Cornelius saga.)

We See No Evil (Book 4 in the Cornelius saga - *Available for Pre-order. Release date: June 6, 2017*

Haunted Cruise: The Shakedown

Hidden Sins Revealed (A Shocking Serial Killer Thriller)

Do we know what awaits us on the other side? Is it a blackness or void that we will not be cognizant of – a deafening silence that hums into a realm of nothingness? Or is it another world, a plane or perhaps *several* planes of ethereal life/existence which we are not privy to at this time?

Whatever you or I believe is irrelevant now. What matters is what the patients of Merci Hospital believe after entering the impeccably reputable facility that, for ages, has been one of physical and emotional healing, rejuvenation and restoration.

One

Don Mather had the look of terror on his face as he dashed down the long, dark corridor; his white hospital gown swaying against his knees. Glancing behind again for probably the fifth time, he could see the hunger in their piercing eyes, the thirst in their pasty skin and they were closing in on him. Don's legs that had run many sprints back in the early eighties at Forrest High school and had won gold medals for his track team during senior year, couldn't seem to outrun those who were obviously intent upon his capture.

Strangely enough, he could barely feel his legs, but he knew they were there and he was using them, just as he used his right hand to forcefully tilt over the narrow, oxygen tank in a corner before the bend and he could hear it rolling behind him. However, another glance assured him that it had not accomplished its intended mission. None of his pursuers seemed to have been slowed one bit.

"Leave me the hell alone!" He yelled as he swung to the left down another long hallway, tossing down an IV drip machine that felt weightless to the touch, similar to how the oxygen tank had felt. The crew on the chase seemed unfazed by Don's cries and escape tactics.

The entire hospital had an icy air about it – not in temperature, but in sensation. Don remembered thinking that right after he caught himself hovering backwards against the ceiling, peering down at his partially-clad body laid out on the stretcher, and watching only for a brief time, Jill, his wife of eleven years, screaming her lungs out after he had flat-lined. "How could this be?" She cried. "He wasn't even sick! What did you people do to him?"

He effortlessly and involuntarily descended to the floor and by the pull of some unfamiliar force, was led to walk out of the massive room and into the long, wide corridor. That's when the "color thing" really hollered at him, even more so than before. Everywhere he looked was colorless and the entire atmosphere instigated a somber feel with an achy sense of loss. He could see the Triage Room straight ahead and as he slowly proceeded down the corridor, he realized that perhaps *colorless* was not the appropriate word for what he was observing. Perhaps, it was more "dull gray" than just "colorless".

Nothing made sense to Don. These current series of events all felt surreal as medical personnel who busied about and fellow patients being cared for walked to and fro, passing him as if he wasn't even there. For some reason, he dared not get anyone's attention. After all, he knew he was on his way to somewhere special although he had no idea *where*.

Within what felt like minutes, the corridor grew darker and darker – not black, but a deeper hue of gray, and people walking about suddenly disappeared. Don stopped and looked around. No one was left. With a sudden rise in anxiety, he wondered what in the world just happened. Not like the whole deal wasn't already strange enough.

"Hello!" He cried out, hearing nothing but a slight echo in return. He called out a second time and waited, but the same thing happened. Fear was beginning to slither its nasty way inside of him like a yard snake in a hole. He wanted nothing more than to wake up from this awful nightmare. To do just that, he pinched himself, but soon realized this was no dream of the frightening kind, but a discomfiting reality. Don decided to walk on, then a few steps in, heard a snicker behind him. Quickly glancing around, he was sure he would find the source. An eerie stillness greeted him instead.

I must get back to Jill, he thought, with more clarity than when he had first left the Recovery Room. He recalled she was a total wreck and now that meant something to him – much more than it had before.

He proceeded in the direction from which he had come and after a few steps – two or three – that's when he saw them – a sight which caused the very hairs on the nape of his neck to stand at full attention. Whomever or whatever they were collectively stood from the creeping position they had kept in the corner of the corridor. Don wondered where they had come from; why he had not seen them before, but soon realized that particular corner harbored a shade of some type which appeared to hang just above and around where they had been stooping.

They were advancing toward him very slowly.

"Um... what's going on here?" Don demanded, although he could feel his heart pounding rapidly. "I'm just trying to get back to my room. My wife is there."

He incited no reaction in the slightest from any of them. *They* could have been twenty, thirty or more. Don could not tell. His only concern was their frigid appearance and knowing *come hell or high water,* he was going to get back to Jill. He was confident she could explain this odd series of events. She usually had all the answers whenever things went awry and was so good at making everything better, despite all the times he had messed up.

He heard more snickering among the group, and what sounded like spurts of grunting. Then there was a putrid smell that almost suffocated him as they were closing in.

"What do you want?" Don backed up. "Look, I don't want any trouble. I… I don't know what's going on right now. I'm just here for a surgery."

"Don..."

Someone called his name from the opposite direction. The soft, tender voice sounded feminine, but he couldn't be sure. He knew it wasn't Jill's.

Glancing around, he asked: "Who is that? Who's calling me?" *Maybe it's the nurse who prepped me for surgery,* he thought. He re-focused on the group.

"Don..." it went again.

"Who is it? Where are you?" His head felt like it was about to spin.

Then he heard: "Run! You can escape through the yellow door!"

Yellow door... Don thought. *There's no yellow anything around here.*

The hideous crowd, some with drooling tongues and pitch-black, ophidian eyes, dashed towards him in unison and Don took off down the corridor like a bat out of Hell. Instantaneously, it struck him, though *survival* was at the fore-front of his mind: How was it possible for him to sprint after having suffered the torn ligament in his knee? Did he already have the surgery? And if so, how could he have possibly recovered so quickly? Was he still alive or was he, in fact, dead?

He managed to get a good distance down the corridor, but not much farther from his last turn by the oxygen tank before they finally caught up to him and overpowered him. Their lingering odor at close proximity was insanely torturous, aside from what he suffered as they literally ripped him apart and feasted upon every inch of him.

Two

When Luke Bazard, Merci Hospital's Director, entered the conference room, he met Jill Mather sobbing her eyes out. She was sitting at the oval desk with Dr. Franklyn Radford, Chief of Staff.

"Mrs. Mather..." Bazard extended his hand. "I'm Luke Bazard. I am very sorry for your loss." He sat to her left. "You insisted you wished to speak with me?"

Luke Bazard was a Scottish native who migrated to Cheshire County in Bloomberg more than thirty years earlier. He was of medium build and height, and along with his salt and pepper hair, sported a neat goatee. He had more initials behind his name than the C.E.O., yet was far more humble by most accounts than the semi-retired, majorly braggadocious Carlton Ferrin.

"I want to know..." Jill's voice was breaking as she looked into Bazard's green eyes, "...why my husband is dead."

"Mrs. Mather..." Bazard started.

"I want to know how a healthy young man in his thirties could die after coming here for a simple procedure to his knee. Was it the anesthesia?" She glanced at the doctor, before refocusing on Bazard. "After he went under, he never woke up. How can that be?"

Bazard shifted slightly in his chair and cleared his throat. "Mrs. Mather, I am not trying to sound cold or unsympathetic, but with any surgical procedure, as you and your husband would have been informed before admittance, there are risks involved."

Jill attempted to interject, but Bazard held his hand up abruptly.

"Please allow me to finish," he said. "At this point, his death would have to be properly investigated although right now we can assume what might have happened. However, we cannot share those assumptions because that's exactly what they are – *assumptions*. An autopsy would have to be conducted to get all the answers we need. I'm sorry, ma'am, I cannot imagine the pain you must be in right now, but that's all I'm at liberty to say." He glanced at Dr. Radford who lowered his head slightly. "Again, you have my deepest sympathy." Bazard got up to leave.

Jill glared at him in utter shock. "So, that's it? That's all you have to say? You come in here to give me that little speech and then you just get up to leave? Is that how much the patients of Merci Hospital mean to you?"

"Ma'am, Mr. Bazard came down to speak with you although he is not required to," Dr. Radford said. "You have to be patient and wait for the results of your husband's autopsy."

"Mrs. Mather, I am bound by the hospital's regulations not to speak anymore of this. Protocol must be followed in all cases," Bazard said.

Jill nodded her head and stood up as well. "That's exactly what Don's death is to you people – just another case."

"Mrs. Mather, please..." Bazard was clearly saddened by her remark. "Each and every patient of this hospital is extremely important to all the staff. I didn't mean to infer that your husband was anything but."

Jill dabbed her eyes with the handkerchief and wiped her nose, then started toward the door.

Radford hurried over to open it for her. "Mrs. Mather, please accept my deepest condolences."

She slid the dark shades from the top of her head down to her eyes, and left without uttering another word. As Radford quietly shut the door behind her, Bazard was leaning against the desk.

"This is the fourth death in ten days that we can't give a sensible explanation for," Bazard said softly. "I feel for that lady – for all the families that have suffered such unexpected losses."

"It's all very odd, to say the least." Radford stood nearby. "The autopsies of two of the patients indicated they both died of heart attacks, but I don't know… something just doesn't feel right."

"It can't be the anesthesia," Bazard opined. "Different anesthesiologists have administered different types of anesthesia on those patients, so there's nothing in common as far as that's concerned."

Radford nodded.

"What baffles me is that all four cases involved a simple procedure that wasn't supposed to be life-threatening. Their loved ones thought they'd be discharged the same day. How could this be that their hearts just gave out and they died? It doesn't make sense." He combed his fingers through his hair and sauntered over to the large glass window overlooking the town.

"Radford…"

"Yes, sir?"

"We have to keep whatever's going on around here under wraps. We can't allow this hospital to become the focus of any malpractice investigation. Merci's had an upstanding reputation in this county for more than a century."

"I understand, sir."

"Okay. Good."

Just then, the phone in the center of the otherwise empty desk rang. Bazard picked up.

"Okay," he said. "Let her have a seat in my office. I'm on my way." He looked at Radford while setting the handset in place. "The new nurse our recruiter has highly recommended is here. She'll make her way down to you in E.R. when we're done."

Radford nodded again.

"Just keep a keen eye out on things, Frank, and remember what I said."

"Sure thing, sir."

They both headed for the door.

Three

Catherine Lucene stood up as Bazard entered the spacious, posh office he had occupied for twenty years.

"Good morning, Catherine. It's wonderful to finally meet you! I'm Luke Bazard." He went right over and sealed the greeting with a warm handshake.

"It's a pleasure to meet you too, sir," Catherine replied with a smile.

"Please sit down," Bazard said before taking his seat directly across from her.

Catherine's first thought after entering the room and being in awe of its architectural design, was that the wide, leather chair with the sewn-in metal buttons looked royal enough to seat a king.

"I don't usually get to meet new staff personally as I am always swamped with the running of this hospital," Bazard started, "but I had to make it a point to meet you on your first day here at Merci. Steve, our extremely competent recruiter, raved on and on about you."

Catherine's smile extended a tad wider, yet not without humility. "I am really honored to be a part of this wonderful facility, sir, and thank you so much for your kind words."

Bazard leaned forward. "I can't imagine a nurse coming so far within such a short space of time. I understand you hold two degrees?"

"Yes, sir. I'm a CPA, but while in college working towards my masters in Accounts, I was pulled towards healthcare. I finished up my studies in order to become the accountant my mom expected me to be since I love Math, then I pursued my Nursing degree."

"That's rather commendable. Is there a particular reason you felt pulled, as you say, towards health care?"

Catherine's long, slender legs were crossed and her fingers loosely interlaced atop her lap. "I was engaged to this wonderful guy while in college. His name was Brice. He proposed to me during my junior year and we had plans to marry after we got our degrees. The problem was he had Sickle Cell Anemia. Because of it, he struggled throughout high school and in college, but he was a fighter – determined to do whatever he set his mind to." Catherine could see Bazard's genuine interest in the story. "Well, a year before we were both set to graduate, his disease worsened and eventually, he ended up in a coma. I remember looking at him in his hospital bed with all these machines attached that were just barely keeping him alive. I wished with everything inside of me that I could do something to turn it all around; to help him; to wake him up and hear his voice again. I agonized over my inability to help him, but there was nothing I could do. He passed away one week before our graduation."

Bazard could tell by the tears Catherine tried to restrain that Brice's death still affected her. "I'm so sorry to hear that, Catherine." He cleared his throat. "I can certainly see now why the healthcare profession appealed to you."

"I just wanted to be able to help people who are sick; to do what I can to make them better. That's why I went back to college and studied Nursing."

"How did your mother feel about that? You said she wanted you to become an accountant."

"Technically, I did become an accountant. She can't say I didn't." Catherine smiled.

Bazard laughed. "Yeah, you're right."

"Mom's thing was she wanted me to use my gifts and talents throughout life. She always said that's what we're all called to do and that way, we live a good life, and I agree with her to a large extent. She also understood my desire to be a nurse and encouraged me in that as well. Mom was worried at first that I might not be able to afford my own apartment and car because she didn't know nurses make a pretty decent living."

Bazard couldn't hold back his laughter. "Sounds like your mother is a very special gal."

"She surely is. She and my dad are living it up in California, especially now since I've proven to them fifteen years ago that I can pay my own rent and actually afford a car."

"Well, it's nice of you to have shared your personal story with me, Catherine, and it's amazing how one thing, though tragic, led you into the medical field. Steve was elated when we were able to snatch you from Anselm's Hospital. I imagine they were sorry to see you leave."

"The people there were very nice. We got on well in the twelve years I worked there as Head Nurse. When I was offered a job here and even told they would create a position for me based on my qualifications, I knew I couldn't turn it down. Merci's reputation, not only in the State, but in this country, speaks for itself."

"We only seek out the best!" Bazard said. "And we do what we can to get them."

"I'm flattered, sir."

"You're too modest, Catherine." He stood to his feet. "I won't keep you any longer. Dr. Peters, who assists Dr. Radford, is expecting you. As you were told, you'll be working periodically with Radford as his department is just one of the areas you will work in as per the rotation method we implemented for you. We know you'd be perfect in Administration, but since you insisted on getting hands on with patients as you've always been, we graciously oblige."

Standing now as well, Catherine said, "I truly appreciate this opportunity, Mr. Bazard. I'll do my best to meet your expectations."

"Just continue to do what you've been doing prior to coming here, giving one hundred percent, and I am sure that will be good enough."

"Yes, sir."

Bazard escorted her out of the office and she was met by Dr. Ron Peters, who would accompany her downstairs to the ER. The two had met a week earlier when she was there to sign the contract and insurance documents.

"Great to have you onboard," Peters said as they headed to the elevator.

"I'm glad to be here," Catherine replied.

"I must say, your impending arrival has been the topic of discussion around here for a while."

"Really?" The elevator doors closed.

"When Mr. Bazard speaks, everyone around here listens, and he's been literally boasting about how Merci was able to snatch one of the best medical professionals in the county."

Catherine grinned.

"No, no. That's a big deal!" Peters asserted.

Bazard doesn't get too involved in the hiring process. He leaves that to Steve and the others in HR. But for some reason, he's been really running his mouth about you and I have to admit – for good reason. Your reputation precedes you. Heard you were able to save more than a few lives when the patients were practically given up on."

Catherine looked at him. "You heard all that?"

"Have I?" He smirked. "Who hasn't?!"

"Catherine!" A nurse exclaimed after Catherine and Dr. Peters left the elevator. Mae Fields was around Catherine's age, but looked a lot older due to her thinning, gray hair.

The ladies embraced warmly. "Mae, it's great to see you!" Catherine said. "I haven't set eyes on you since college!"

"It's been sixteen years this June, huh?"

"I presume you girls know each other," Peters interjected.

"Know? We were roommates in college and hung out practically all the time," Mae said. "That is, in between wrecking our brains for exams and whenever Brice gave you a breathing moment!" Seeing the smile quickly vanish from Catherine's face, Mae instantly wished she had put her foot in her mouth instead. I'm sorry, Catherine. I didn't mean to..."

"It's okay; really. It's been almost two decades. I'm fine," Catherine tried to sound convincing.

Peters was confused, but chose not to pry.

"Silly me! Are you sure?" Mae sought assurance.

"Yes, I'm sure!" Catherine hugged her again. "So, you work here in ER, huh?" They were in an area closed off by a one-sided see-through glass on the opposite end of where patients registered.

"Yes, I do."

Mae had only been employed at Merci for about five years. She had returned to her hometown after giving up residency in France where she migrated a year after graduation. She lived there with a cousin who regularly boasted of the city life in Paris.

Dr. Peters soon took Catherine to meet with Dr. Radford, then on a tour of the hospital. Catherine spent most of the day prepping for what was to be her first official "work day", beginning the following morning.

* * *

Catherine picked up on the third ring.

"How's the new job?" Amy asked. They had been best friends since grade school.

"So far, so good." Catherine got comfortable on the couch, the dry dish-cloth still in hand. "After all, how much can go wrong in just one day?"

"Hmm… a little sarcastic tonight, are we? I thought with a new job came a new attitude?"

"Really? How come I didn't notice that with you when you got that high-powered post at Ferndhardt & Stats, the highest paid Accounting firm this side of the region?"

"You didn't notice? I thought everyone did." Amy chuckled.

"Girl, you are too much. Seriously though, I know this is gonna be my best job yet. I can't say I have much to complain about where I came from, but Merci Hospital is a step up, for sure. I met the Director, Mr. Bazard today. He's really nice."

"*You* met the Director? Do all nurses get to meet the Director of Merci?" Amy asked.

"Apparently not."

"Well, my girl ain't playin'. How about we meet for lunch tomorrow since we're now working just down the street from one another?"

"I'm assigned to night shift the first week." Catherine said. "Maybe we can arrange something later on. It isn't always easy breaking for lunch. You know how that is."

"Cat, please promise me you'll do better taking care of yourself than you did at Anselm's."

"I really don't have time for another lecture tonight, Amy. I was in the middle of making sushi." Catherine tossed the dish-cloth across her shoulder.

"I'm serious, Catherine."

Catherine knew Amy only called her *Catherine* when she meant business.

"You push yourself way too hard sometimes. You don't need to have another dizzy spell and faint like you did before."

"Must you always bring that up? I told you already I hadn't eaten for hours, thus the reason for the light-headedness. It's been two years since that happened, it's never happened since and you're still bringing it up!"

"I'm just concerned. That's all."

"I know you are, babes, but there's no need to worry your pretty little head about me. I'm in great health and perfectly fine. But listen, I gotta run now. Gotta finish dinner. I'm starving."

Four

At 8:28 p.m., Catherine left the small kitchen on her ward to do rounds. She had just finished sipping a cup of coffee and felt rejuvenated to take on the last three and a half hours of her shift.

The Female Medical Ward was quiet, as was the norm that time of night. As a veteran nurse, she always loved the night shift, especially if she had been stationed somewhere other than in the ER. She was approaching the end of her first week there and would be on day shift the following morning.

Walking along the wide corridor, she stopped by some of the rooms to check in.

"You say I should what? What?"

Catherine heard eighty-year-old Agatha Dempsey speaking aloud in her room. She had been admitted two days earlier after suffering severe food poisoning.

"Oh, okay. Just give me a minute. Don't leave. I'm coming right now."

Catherine twisted the door handle and immediately saw Agatha rip the IV needle out of her arm and was attempting to get up. "Mrs. Dempsey, you can't do that!" Catherine exclaimed, dashing over to the woman's bed. "Let me fix that for you."

Agatha looked at Catherine with those big, blue eyes that had lured many men in her younger days. "No need to bother, dear. The nice man over there said it's time to go. Isn't he handsome?"

Catherine looked in the direction of Agatha's stare. "What man are you talking about?"

"Can't you see him? He's wearing that nice, black suit and those shiny, pointed shoes." She then whispered, "He's a real looker, ain't he?"

"Mrs. Dempsey, you must lie back down and get your rest." Catherine lifted Agatha's legs onto the bed, then went to re-attach the IV.

"Ok. I'll be ready." Agatha smiled, looking toward the northern side of the wall. "I can't wait!" She rubbed her hands together like a teenager.

Catherine was convinced the old lady was partially senile or may have a touch of Alzheimer's.

"All set," Catherine told her. "I need you to not bother with your drip anymore. You want to get better, not worse. Right?"

By then, Agatha was no longer staring at the wall. "I will be much better soon, dear. The nice gentleman told me as much. He said they're waiting for me. Isn't that wonderful? He promised we're leaving tonight."

"Really?"

Agatha nodded quickly. "Yeah. Yeah. Guess who else I saw?" She asked eagerly.

"Who?" Catherine wasn't sure she wanted the answer.

"I saw Uncle Rubin! He looked just the same as I saw him last time when he was in that lovely cream-colored coffin. The undertaker did a marvelous job with his remains after he was nearly mangled in that warehouse."

Catherine grimaced.

"You see, they say it was a freak accident where the rolling machine he was operating malfunctioned. When he climbed up on it and tried to fix it, it started up at high speed. He slipped in between and it nearly chewed him to bits. He was only able to hold on to dear life a few days after that. Poor Uncle Rubin."

"Wow. I'm so sorry to hear that," Catherine said, convinced that Agatha was a real screw up.

"Thanks, but no thanks, dear. I say that 'cause... he's in Heaven now. No place else I'd rather be. That's for sure."

Catherine managed a brief smile. "I have to finish my rounds now. Is there anything else I can do for you before I go?"

Agatha thought for a moment. "When my daughter, Lily, comes to see me tomorrow, tell her I said I love her very much and that I saw her great Uncle Rubin."

"I'm sure you'd be able to tell her that yourself, Mrs. Dempsey." Catherine straightened her pillow. "You have a good sleep. We'll be checking on you later."

"Good night, dear. I'm going to sleep soon, so don't you worry. Go on home and get your beauty rest. You young girls need your beauty rest so paper bags won't form under your perfect eyes."

"Yes, ma'am." Catherine smiled as she shut the door behind her. Immediately, she headed back to the Nurse's station and alerted the ladies on duty to keep an eye on Agatha since the senior had taken the liberty to rip the IV right out of her arm.

2:58 a.m...

Having been checked on by another nurse twice since Catherine settled her back in, Agatha tossed the covers from her legs and sat straight up. Her little legs dangled over the side of the bed. She stood up and slipped on her bright blue, feathery bedroom slippers and slowly pulled the IV machine along with her as she made her way to the northern side of the room.

"Uh huh." She nodded as she stood in front of the wall. She looked down at the needle in her forearm. "I see." And then at the wall again. "Are you sure? Okay. If that's what it would take." She removed the tape covering the needle in her arm which was connected to the IV and slowly pulled out the long needle, grimacing a bit this time as opposed to the first time. She faced the wall again as she elevated the needle to her throat, and sticking it forcefully some centimeters into the left front side of her neck, she ripped across to the right with a strength unnatural of a woman her size and age, and without a wince. Blood gushed out and Agatha slumped to the floor; the IV machine crashing down as she fell against it.

A doctor passing the room heard the commotion and hurried inside. He found Agatha bleeding and hollered for assistance as he tried his best to help her.

Agatha was standing quietly nearby looking down at her frail body and at the doctor working feverishly to save her life. Two nurses rushed in to assist.

"We're losing her!" The doctor exclaimed.

"A...ga...tha..." The little, old lady heard the faintest voice.

Lured toward the doorway, she passed straight through and into the corridor.

"I'm coming!" She said. "Where are you? I don't see you anywhere." She proceeded further down. "Is that you, Uncle Rubin? You're taking me up there now to mom and dad, and Aunt Gretchen, and the others? It's been such a long time since I've seen them all."

Midway through the corridor, Agatha was struck by how much darker everything had suddenly become, and a worried expression flashed across her face. She stopped in her tracks and looked back.

"Uncle Rubin..."

Thirty seconds passed, then someone replied, "He's not here."

She turned around immediately, but didn't see anyone. There was something about the strange voice that made her uneasy.

"Where is he, then? Might this be the nice, young man I saw before? Is it you – the handsome one?"

Someone appeared twenty feet in front of her. The image was vague almost, but the individual's height is what caused her to smile. "It's you." She sighed. "I was beginning to get worried."

The man stood silently.

"Is there something wrong? I can't see your face that good, but I can... almost see straight through you."

The man turned around slowly and walked off.

"Um... excuse me, young man. Where are you going?" Agatha called behind him. She was beginning to get that worried feeling again, and this time an eerie sensation was making its way up her throat. "Where is my Uncle Rubin? He was supposed to be here. Where has he gone?" She started behind the stranger, but no matter how fast she tried to walk and how slowly he appeared to be moving, the space between them didn't seem to be closing in.

The corridor got darker and darker until Agatha was overcome with pitch darkness. She became paralyzed with fear.

"One, two they're coming for you..." The voice sounded like that of a child.

Three, four they'll settle the score..."

"Who... who is that? What score? What're you talking about?" Agatha insisted.

"Five, six, you were full of tricks..."

Agatha put her hand to her chest. "What tricks? I don't know what you're talking about." She stated it emphatically, but her conscience knew the opposite to be true. She had flashbacks of poor, old Gus Thornton, her third husband of twelve years – the unlucky bastard that had gotten pissy drunk every night the whole time she knew him. She saw that rat poison she tossed inside his food that fateful Sunday afternoon and how it worked wonders inside his already unhealthy body. She also saw that big, fat life insurance check of two hundred and fifty thousand with her name on it; the brand, new Cadillac, flashy jewelry and fancy clothes. Yeah, in that dark corridor that night, the memories of her so-called "trick" flashed before her.

Agatha started to panic. She knew she couldn't be alive any longer after slitting her throat and realized for the first time that she had made a terrible mistake. "I… I did it. I did it! Okay? He didn't deserve it, but I want to live again. Give me a chance to live again. I promise, I'll go back and give what's left of the money to his daughters. I'm so sorry."

"Seven, eight… it's WAY too late!" A loud, sepulchral voice shook her to the core.

"Please, I beg you, let me go back!"

The thick blanket of darkness began to dissipate and to her immense relief, Agatha could see clearly again. However, she found herself in a different place. It appeared to be the inside of an operating room.

"What am I doing here?" She muttered under her breath.

"Sphh!"

Agatha looked around, her heart pulsating with fear.

"You must find the yellow door. That's the only way you'll make it out." It was a feminine voice.

Agatha was confused. "Make it out? What are you saying? Where are you?"

Suddenly, the room exploded with a classical symphony. Trumpets, piano, violins, a female vocalist with a powerful, resonant voice could be heard. Then it stopped as quickly as it started and a team of men in long, white jackets appeared around the operating table. Several more people wearing blue scrubs appeared and were soon focusing on the young woman who screamed in agony as they worked on her.

Agatha stood silently from a distance watching an apparent surgery in progress. No one seemed to notice that she was even in the room.

"Scalpel!" A doctor called out.

"No!" The patient vehemently protested.

"Julie, we have to get it out. Just lie still and try to relax."

"Why aren't we administering anesthesia?" A female nurse asked one of the assisting doctors.

"Because if we do, she'll never wake up. She has an allergic reaction to most of the mainstream anesthetics, which is good in this case because if we put her to sleep, that dreadful thing inside there will hide." He pointed to the girl's stomach.

"So, we're not gonna do anything at all to numb the pain?" The nurse asked in disbelief.

"I'm afraid not."

"Doctor, we all know there are ways around this."

The doctor glanced her way. "Sandra, the patient you see here personally consented to have this procedure performed without any form of anesthesia. Don't mind the screaming. It was her idea."

Momentarily, the nurse was at a loss for words. "There's no way she could have been in her right mind. I can't be a part of this. I'm leaving!" She started to walk off.

"What? At the risk of losing your job?" the doctor asked.

Her two young kids flashing before her, the nurse reluctantly turned around and returned to her post.

"That a girl. Don't worry about anything. Everything here's covered legally."

Agatha watched as a doctor made an incision across the woman's abdomen. The agonizing shrill which followed had an effect on most of those in the room.

"Clamp!"

Another nurse handed him the tool.

"My God!" A nearby doctor quietly exclaimed as his colleague grasped something that wiggled. Gripping the forceps tightly, he carefully removed a live two-foot snake that had found its home in the woman's body.

The hollering hadn't ceased, though it lessened somewhat after the incision had been made.

"Is it out?" she asked. "Is that bastard out of me?"

"Here it is," the doctor showed her as the skinny reptile dangled in the clutch of his surgical tool.

Agatha, still in silent observance in the corner, instantly covered her mouth.

The patient grimaced at the sight of the creature. "To think it was growing inside me the whole time! I'll get that effin' witch! She'll wish she'd never messed with me!"

Nurse Sandra, who wanted to leave, shook her head; shocked at what she was witnessing.

An assistant nurse had a jar waiting in which the doctor dropped the snake and it was immediately sealed.

They went to work stitching up the woman and although her face marked excruciating pain, all appeared to be going well until suddenly, she began hemorrhaging on the table and her eyes rolled to the back of her head. Everyone flew into "panic mode", frantically working to fix the situation. Regardless of all attempts to stop the hemorrhaging, their efforts were quickly appearing futile.

Amazingly from her position, Agatha could see the heart monitor and hear its rhythmic beats. But soon, a series of alarms started going off and the young woman flat-lined.

"Hand me the paddles, dammit!" The doctor demanded. He snatched them and got to work right away trying to restart the patient's heart, knowing fully well that there was no hope.

"I knew this was a bad idea!" A young nurse exclaimed. "We've done this! We've done this."

"I told you I wanted no part of this!" Sandra reminded the doctor standing next to her.

He did not respond. She could see the heaving of his chest.

Minutes later, the patient, declared dead, was covered with a sheet.

"Now, we're all in trouble!" Sandra said.

"No, we're not!" The chief surgeon replied, putting the paddles down. "This lady consented to the procedure. It's in black and white."

"Even so, are we not morally culpable – to allow a patient to tell us how to run things in the operating room?" Sandra returned.

"We saw that creature inside of her on the x-ray. It had been sucking the very life out of her. If we didn't extract it, she wouldn't have survived anyway. She wanted it out and we helped her."

"These are not the old days when anesthesia wasn't available, Doctor. We conducted a major surgery without anesthetics of any kind. None! Absolutely none! No wonder her body went into shock. What did any one of you expect?" She looked at them standing there. "I knew it would happen. That's why I didn't want to be here."

"No one put a gun to your head, Sandra." Another doctor interjected.

"No, not an actual gun, but Doctor Pintard here pointed a verbal one." She glared at him. "If shit hits the fan, I'm telling you all now, I'm covering my ass. To hell with all of you. If it means me losing my job, so be it! As far as I'm concerned, this was murder. This went against everything we swore to uphold."

She stormed out of the room and Agatha saw the scene fade to black. She was alone again in the operating room, still rattled by the unfolding of strange events she understood had taken place sometime earlier.

"Hello..." she cried. "I want to leave here, please. I need to find my Uncle Rubin."

"What about me?" A different voice from before answered her.

Agatha turned to her left and threw her hand to her chest. "Gus?"

The man, just an inch or two taller than she was, appeared in the doorway. "It's me," he calmly replied, approaching her.

"Gus, I didn't mean to..."

"Shhh. Say nothing, my lollipop." He rested a finger across his lips. "I came to take you away from here."

"You did?"

"Yes, sweetheart."

Agatha noticed the same emptiness in Gus's eyes that was there all those years he had drunk himself into a stupor. They always appeared glassy and to her, it meant he had no soul. When he was alive, that characteristic never frightened her, not the way it did that night seeing him again three years after his concealed murder. She felt a lump in her throat. "I don't wanna go with you, Gus. I'm waiting for my uncle."

"Your uncle? You mean... him?" He looked to their right; Agatha's eyes followed.

Faced with terror, she emitted a blood-curdling scream. "No! No! Go away! You're not him! You are not my Uncle Rubin!"

"But he is." Gus was smiling as the sinewy, headless beast with a tight collar around its hollow neck, slowly approached. It appeared four-legged, although it was advancing on two.

"This is not my Uncle Rubin! Gus, you know my Uncle Rubin." She backed up closer to her dead husband. "Please, make him go away! I don't want him anywhere near me."

"But this is who you saw before you came here -- before you joined us. You agreed to come," Gus explained.

"You're wrong. I never saw this thing!"

Gus looked at the creature and arched a brow. "Show her."

Standing even closer to Gus, Agatha watched as the dreadful thing evolved in front of her very eyes to the image of her Uncle Rubin, then moments later, returned to its true nature.

She shook her head in disbelief. "This can't be real. None of this is real!"

Gus leaned his head to the side, looking at her with a tad of compassion. "Are you ready to go, my love?"

Agatha glanced at him, then looked back at the beast now only inches away from her. "Yes! Yes, I'll go with you!" She said eagerly.

Gus extended his hand and with reluctance, she placed hers inside of his and they walked off together, exiting the room into an open area that resembled a long, desolate road. Agatha glanced behind and noticed the God-forsaken beast was gone.

As they walked along, hand-in-hand, like they had done early on in their marriage, Agatha looked at Gus and asked, "Where are we going, Gus? Where are you taking me?"

With his focus straight ahead and his grip of her wrinkled hand instantly tightening, he calmly replied, "Straight to Hell, my love. Straight to Hell."

Screaming and struggling to get away, Agatha was led a little further down the path, then there was a sudden drop. She felt the intensity of the flames and smelt burning and decaying flesh long before she ever hit the ground below.

Five

When Catherine arrived at work the following morning, Mae hurried over to her.

"Did you hear what happened last night?" Mae asked.

"No. What happened?" Catherine was concerned.

"A patient died."

"Mae, this is a hospital. Unfortunately, sometimes people do die here."

Mae shook her head. "You don't understand. This person killed herself."

"What? Who was it?" Mae had Catherine's full attention.

"She was in Female Medical. An elderly lady named Dempsey."

"Agatha Dempsey?"

"That's right." Mae nodded.

Feeling weak in her knees, Catherine found a chair. "My God. She knew she was going to die last night. I didn't take her seriously. I never thought for a second she actually planned to kill herself."

Mae was surprised by the revelation. "What'd she say?"

"She just kept talking about a man who promised to take her to her Uncle Robert or somebody. She was talking out of her head. She even ripped out her IV last night. The nurses had to keep a close eye on her."

"Apparently, she did the same thing later on, but used the needle itself to cut her own throat."

Shocked, Catherine asked, "She did what?"

Mae nodded. "What an unusual way to end your life, huh? What beats me is how she even had the nerve to endure the pain to cut so deeply."

"I can't believe this," Catherine muttered. "I just can't believe this!" Just then, she remembered something. "Has her daughter been here already?"

"I wasn't here, but it sounded like she was alerted to her mother's passing early this morning."

"So, it happened this morning?"

"Uh huh. In the wee hours."

Catherine got up. "I must contact her daughter."

"Why?"

"Mrs. Dempsey gave me a message for her."

* * *

Lily Dempsey arrived at the hospital an hour before Catherine's shift ended.

Catherine met her in the Waiting Room and invited her to the cafeteria for a short chat. They sat at a table at the back. The middle-aged woman appeared to have been deeply broken by the news of her mother's passing.

"I agree this is a bit unusual for a nurse to do with the relative of a patient, but I guess for me, people might figure it's the norm."

Lily was looking at her rather blankly.

"I wanted to give you a message from your mother."

The woman's face seemed to come alive. "Are you psychic or something?"

"No. It's nothing like that!" Catherine said. It even was a tad insulting as she didn't like so-called psychics, believing they were nothing more than a bunch of relentless fraudsters trying to trick the hopelessly naive out of their hard-earned cash. "I saw your mother last night before I went home. She was acting kind of... strange." Catherine paused.

"Strange... in what way?" Lily asked.

"She was talking to herself; holding a real conversation. Did she ever do that?"

Lily grimaced. "No. I've never known her to do that."

Catherine expected a different answer. "Well, she was talking to herself and said she would be leaving with someone who would take her to her

Uncle Robert, I think. I can't remember the name for sure, but it started with R."

"It must've been Rubin she was referring to. As far as I know, she doesn't have an Uncle Robert."

"That's it! *Rubin.*"

Lily sighed. "She hadn't mentioned his name in years, but she loved him a great deal. Said he was her favorite uncle on her dad's side."

"I don't know… she seemed really keen about it," Catherine said. "She even told me to tell you she loved you very much."

On hearing those words, Lily broke down in tears and Catherine reached across the table for her hand.

"I'm sorry. I had no idea she planned to end her life."

Lily tried to regain her composure. "We don't know for sure if that's what happened."

"What do you mean?" Catherine was perplexed.

"We're not sure that someone else didn't come in and do that to her."

"Mrs. Dempsey, I can't..."

"I know you can't wander into that arena with me, Nurse. I don't expect you to. I've requested a thorough investigation into this matter, but I really didn't have to because I'm certain the police are already conducting their own. I'm a lawyer. I'm aware of procedure."

Catherine pressed her hands against the front of her skirt. "Well, I just wanted to share with you the message your mother wanted me to pass on. I'm truly sorry for your loss." She got up.

Lily stood as well. "I'm so glad you did. My mother was a beautiful person who loved me unconditionally. I'm an only child; I was her whole world and she was mine." Catherine could see the tears on the verge of gushing again. "I'm hoping in my heart that this is something other than suicide, even though the other possibility is also horrible. Either way, I've lost her and she's not coming back. My only comfort would be in knowing that now she's with her beloved Uncle Rubin and her parents who were all so wonderful."

Catherine smiled.

She walked Lily back to the Waiting Room and watched as she exited the front door of the hospital.

Six

Three weeks later…

"That Dempsey death has finally been ruled a suicide," Dr. Radford said to Catherine after inviting her to his office. "The nerve of her daughter to entertain the possibility of it being anything else! The woman's fingerprints were found on the needle."

"It's good to know the truth," Catherine replied.

"For sure." Radford crossed his legs. "I wanted you to know, Catherine, that you're doing a wonderful job. But of course, we knew what we were getting."

"Thank you, sir. That's very nice of you."

"Well then, let me not hold you up. I hear Dr. Diggis has asked for you to assist him in the Theater for a procedure in a couple of hours, huh?"

"Yes, sir. A little girl is coming in for an appendectomy." Catherine stood up.

"That's good. Simple procedure. Will you be coming out to the annual sporting event we're having at six this evening? It'll be held right here on a section of the hospital's grounds."

"I'm afraid I won't be able to make it today. Have other plans."

"Okay. Well, probably you'll get to pop by or even participate one day this week before the event closes."

"Perhaps." She smiled.

* * *

"Hello There!" Catherine knelt in front of the seven-year-old, blue-eyed blonde with dimpled cheeks. The child's mother was standing nearby as her daughter clutched a fluffy, white teddy bear. "Are you ready?" Catherine asked.

The girl nodded.

"Now, that's not good manners, Priscilla," her mother, Tonya Abney said in her country accent. "You answer the nice nurse properly."

"Yes, ma'am," Priscilla said.

"Oh, that's quite all right. She's probably not in real *talking mood* right now," Catherine said. "It's expected, considering the circumstances. But everything's going to be just fine!" She told Priscilla. "You'll be all done and back home in no time."

"Ya hear that, honey?" Tonya asked. "Isn't that wonderful?"

"Yes," the little girl answered.

"Okay. Let's go prep for the procedure. I have a bag full of goodies ready for you to take home when it's all over."

The child's eyes alighted with anticipation. "You do?"

Her mother was smiling.

63

"I surely do!" Catherine said, taking her by the hand.

As the orderly and Catherine wheeled Priscilla toward the operating room, her mother walked along, stopping in front of the tall double doors. She leaned over and gave the child a kiss. "I love you, darling. See you in a little while, okay?"

Priscilla nodded. "I love you too, Mommy."

Catherine gave Tonya an assuring smile before they headed inside. Arms folded and wishing she could be there with her daughter, Tonya sauntered over to the waiting room and sat down.

Dr. Kirk Diggis was already inside the Theater with Elvis Graham, the anesthesiologist, and his male assistant.

"What have we here?" Diggis smiled at Priscilla whose lovely locks had been covered by a white cloth cap. "Ready to get this thing done, so you can have those goodies Nurse Catherine has for you?"

"Yes, sir."

"There's no time to waste then. Nurse Catherine explained to you what will happen?"

"You will put me to sleep for a little while, then I'll wake up and I'll be all done!" She raised both hands excitedly.

"You're absolutely right," Diggis replied. "Now, this nice gentleman here, Dr. Graham, will be the one to give you the *sleepy thing*, all right?"

"Okay."

Dr. Graham took a minute to explain to Priscilla what he would be doing. "Before you know it, you'll be fast asleep."

As the doctor administered the anesthesia, Catherine held the little girl's hand. Her face was the last thing Priscilla saw.

Seven

Two hours later…

Catherine's heart was racing as both doctors tried to wake Priscilla.

"The medicine should have worn off a long time ago," Graham said with a tinge of worry on his face.

"You think you might've mistakenly administered too much?" Catherine heard Diggis ask softly.

Graham shook his head, glancing at his assistant. "There's no way."

"He's right," the male nurse verified. "The proper dosage was used. It's recorded right here." He referred to a log book.

"Doctor?" Catherine sought a solution from Diggis.

He sighed deeply. "Our concern is not just that she isn't awake yet, but since her heart beat has slowed considerably, I don't want to move her to the recovery room. We have to run some tests to see exactly what's going on."

Catherine glanced at the sleeping child.

"I'll be right back," Diggis said.

Tonya Abney was at the door when he walked out. She had been pacing the floor for the better part of an hour. "Doctor, what's going on in there? The procedure was supposed to last for about half an hour? Is my baby all right?"

Diggis could not hide his concern. "Mrs. Abney..." he led her over to a private area, "...your daughter has not yet awoken from the anesthesia, so we're running some tests to hopefully see what's going on." He didn't think it appropriate to mention anything else at that point.

Surprised by his disclosure, Tonya asked, "Was the anesthesia too much for her?"

"No, ma'am. Rest assured, the amount administered was the correct amount for your little girl's procedure."

"Well, why isn't she awake then? Did the surgery go well?"

"We've had no obvious complications with the Appendectomy. Just allow us a little more time to find out what's going on and I'll let you know the moment we find out anything. Okay?" He patted her shoulder. "Just try to relax. Your daughter is in good hands."

"All right, Doctor," Tonya replied. She went to sit down again as the doctor hurried on his way.

* * *

Diggis, Graham, Catherine and several other medical professionals were looking at x-rays and scans which all failed to reveal the cause of Priscilla's prolonged sedation. She had not suffered a stroke, ruptured artery nor any brain injury. And other tests came up *negative* for blood clots. The little girl had entered an unexplained comatose state, now sustained by respirators.

Dr. Diggis revealed the distressing news in its entirety to her mother, who upon hearing it could barely hold herself together.

"We will have to monitor what's going on with your daughter," he said. "This is all very unusual, but we know an explanation lies somewhere. We just need some more time to find it. I am very sorry."

After Diggis left, Catherine approached Tonya who was sitting with her hands on her face sobbing.

"Miss Abney, I am so sorry," Catherine said, sitting next to her. "I'm sure Priscilla will be just fine."

"What could've possibly gone wrong?" Tonya's eyes pleaded for the answer. "It was supposed to be a simple procedure. How complicated could it be to remove a little girl's appendix?"

Catherine wasn't sure of what to say. "We'll get to the bottom of this and before you know it, your daughter will be home with you up and running around."

"You told her before she knew it, it would all be over and she'd be home. And she was looking forward to those goodies you promised her."

Catherine felt a wave of guilt wash over her.

"What if she never wakes up?"

"Don't even think that way, Mrs. Abney. You have to be optimistic and not entertain any negative thoughts. Priscilla needs your strength to help her through, so no matter how difficult it is for you, you must stay strong and be confident that your precious child will wake up really soon."

Tonya looked off into nowhere.

"Did you call your husband, Mrs. Abney? I don't think you should be alone much longer."

"My husband and I are separated," she replied. "Have been for a few years. He's not looked back at our daughter after he found a new 'squeeze' more than two years ago. I have nothing to say to him."

"I'm sorry," Catherine said.

"Don't be. It's not like it's the first time. Priscilla and I were always third or fourth place in his life. For a long time, I've had to contend with all his mistresses – the brazen ones that call the wife at home and boast about how many times they've been with Jim. One, in particular, was the worst. That slut tried to even run me off the road, but I fixed her business all right. Six months later, that relationship between her and my husband was over and done with permanently."

Tonya sensed the subject might have been a bit uncomfortable for Catherine. "I'm sorry I bored you with all my woes. What's your name again?" she asked.

"Catherine."

"You are a really nice person, Catherine. Please make sure they do what needs to be done to help my Priscilla. She's all I've got."

Catherine gave her hand a gentle squeeze. "I will. I promise. I'll see you tomorrow, okay?"

"Okay," Tonya replied softly.

As Catherine walked off, she felt awful that she would be going home that evening and Priscilla could not.

* * *

"Follow me," Mae said to Catherine.

They went into the ladies' room nearby – one of several bathrooms sectioned off for medical personnel only.

Mae checked all the cubicles. "Coast clear!" She saw the weariness on Catherine's face. "Are you okay?"

"No. Not really." Catherine sighed. "A little girl came in today for an Appendectomy and is now in a coma. I don't know what happened, Mae. It's been verified that the right type and dosage of anesthesia was used, so it has nothing to do with that. The thing is, we don't know why she hasn't woken up long after the effects would've worn off. I feel terrible right now."

"I heard all about it. It's practically all over the hospital."

"I'm not surprised."

"I have to tell you something Catherine."

Catherine remembered that look in Mae's eyes. She had a similar look the day she broke the news to her that Brice had passed away.

"What?"

"You have to promise me you won't repeat what I'm about to tell you. At least, if you repeat it, don't call my name. You're new here, Catherine, but I've been here for five years and I need this job."

"You have my word, Mae. What is it?"

"There's something weird going on at this hospital. It started happening a couple of weeks before you arrived."

"Something weird? Like what?"

"Patients have been coming here for simple reasons, nothing life-threatening, and after going under have ended up dead."

"Going under. You mean... anesthesia."

Mae nodded. "Precisely."

"Mae..."

"Hear me out. Doctors and nurses all over this hospital know about it – even those in charge like Mr. Bazard. But we've been instructed by our superiors to keep this thing quiet."

Catherine was shocked. "Why would they do that?"

"I think they really don't know what's going on and they don't want to create suspicion or panic which could cause the hospital to be sued by the families of those patients that died. The little girl not waking up is no surprise to many of us. Neither was the man who came in for a simple procedure to his knee who died shortly after he came in. There were others whose deaths we can't explain. But they all went under," Mae said. "Look what happened to Mrs. Dempsey?"

"She wasn't given anesthesia. She killed herself," Catherine said.

"Yeah, but how many people do you know would kill themselves the way she did?"

"What are you saying, Mae?" She folded her arms.

"I'm saying that every day more and more people that come here are dying under mysterious circumstances. Their deaths are being explained away by our superiors and I'm afraid more people will fall victim if something isn't done about it. What if someone we know and love ends up here when we're not around? I'm scared, Catherine. I'm really scared."

"You think someone's sabotaging the anesthesia?"

"I doubt that. Different doctors have been administering different ones. They've even contracted other firms and the same thing has happened, so it isn't likely that it's sabotage," Mae explained.

"I hear you, but none of this makes sense."

"Exactly! Just like the little girl not waking up doesn't make sense either."

Catherine saw her point. "What can we do?"

"I don't know." Mae shook her head. "I just felt I needed to tell you what's going on especially when I heard about what happened to the little girl."

"This is all overwhelming. What in the world have I gotten myself into?"

* * *

Catherine stopped for take-out after work, then went straight home. After a hot shower, she collapsed onto the sofa, watched TV and ate Chinese food. She barely had any appetite as the day's events lingered in her mind.

A little after nine, she switched everything off and went to bed.

Three hours later…

Catherine found herself walking in a long, dark hallway. The whole while, she felt that someone was watching - not just one person, but many. She could feel their piercing stares combined with intense hatred and rage, then suddenly, she sensed a light – not a typical light that brightened a room, but one inside of another. She sensed love and innocence.

A little further in, she thought she saw a glimmer of something straight ahead. It appeared to be a door with a silver frame. Inside was pitch black – a shade of which she had never seen before. Catherine felt drawn to it, satisfied that soon she would be there. She knew she had to pass through.

"Don't pass through!" Someone shouted. "Find the yellow door!"

Something prevented her from moving forward – an invisible barrier. Then from the nothingness, with a pulsating effect, something amazing came into view: Something little; something pale.

"Please help me find the yellow door, Nurse Catherine. I don't see it anywhere," Priscilla said softly. She was standing in front of her.

The child looked extremely sad and sickly, and Catherine could tell she had been crying. Just then, she heard a loud, screeching sound like that of a heavy door or iron gate.

"They're coming to get me!" Priscilla whispered loudly. "I have to find the yellow door before it's too late!" Her sea-blue eyes turned white and Catherine pitched up from her sleep.

She sat up in bed and looked around the room. The events of the dream made her uneasy as it all felt very real.

Eight

8:04 a.m.

Catherine's cell went off just as she pulled into the hospital's parking lot.

"Good morning, super girl," Amy sang. "Calling to find out if we can possibly do lunch today."

Catherine sighed. "I'm not sure about today, Amy. There's so much going on right now, you won't believe."

"So much going on that you can't break for lunch, Catherine?"

Here we go with the 'Catherine' again.

"I usually grab a quick bite at the cafeteria. It's not like I don't eat. I don't take an hour, that's all."

"I hear you, but you're *entitled* to an hour – an hour you can spend with me sometimes."

"It's not like we don't hang out sometimes, Amy, but you win. Let me call you back before noon and I'll let you know for sure, okay?"

"Fair enough," Amy said. "I'll be waiting."

Catherine disconnected and exited the car, locking it with the remote key.

Aware that there had been no change in Priscilla's condition since the day before, Catherine couldn't wait to see her. Watching her little chest rise and fall, she thought of the dream in which the child appeared pleading for help. She couldn't shake the feeling that somehow Priscilla needed her, but just like with Brice, she felt so helpless.

Catherine took Priscilla's hand and gently gripped her fingers. "Priscilla, if you really are reaching out for my help wherever you are, let me know how to help you."

Just then, a message came in over the PA system:

Nurse Catherine Lucene, you're needed at the FMW Reception desk please.

Catherine rested Priscilla's hand at her side and headed out front.

A nurse said, "The lady over there is here to see you. Said it was urgent."

Catherine saw a heavy-set, colored lady approaching.

"Are you Catherine?" She asked.

"Yes. Is there something I can do for you?" She had no idea who the woman was.

"I believe there is. My name is Mary Jenkins. May I speak with you for a minute – outside if you don't mind? I promise, I'm not here for any funny business. It's very important."

Reluctantly, Catherine went over to the reception desk to let them know she'd be outside for only a few minutes.

The women stood a few feet away from the front door near a rail that encircled the western and northern sides of the building.

"I didn't know your surname when I asked for you," the lady started. "I just knew your first name and that the surname started with 'l'. I guess you couldn't have been too hard to find, huh?" She chuckled.

"Ma'am, I really have to get back to work in a minute. What's this about?" Catherine was straight to the point.

"Miss Catherine, I know how you feel about people like me..."

"Wait, I'm not prejudiced!" Catherine interjected.

"I didn't mean prejudiced." The lady chuckled again.

"I know how you feel about sensitives or psychics. I am a psychic."

Catherine shook her head. "Look, I don't have time for any of this stuff." She started to walk off.

"Miss Catherine, Priscilla needs you!" Mary said.

Catherine stopped immediately, then went back. "What do you know about Priscilla?"

"What I'm about to tell you is gonna sound like a truckload of nonsense, but I assure you, every word is true."

"I'm listening."

"L'il Priscilla is trapped inside a plane, parallel to ours. She's there due to no fault of her own. Her momma's to blame."

Catherine listened intently.

"She went under, right?"

Catherine nodded.

"As much as they try and cover up what's going on in this place, it's no secret to me. I can't save the world and I know they won't listen to me anyway, no matter what I told them, but I know you have a heart for L'il Priscilla and as crazy as I sound right now, I know you'll listen. Priscilla needs to go free."

"Help me understand. What is this *plane*?"

"I guess it's more like a portal," Mary said. "It exists because of a curse that started when a wife went to a voodoo priest to cast a spell on the woman who was sleeping with her husband. The spell came in the form of a serpent supernaturally implanted in the woman's abdomen. While there, for months it grew and fed off the blood supply of its host."

Catherine was grimacing as she pictured it.

"The woman came to this very hospital to see what had been causing her severe anemia and nausea, among other symptoms, and they found out by way of an x-ray that there was a fairly long snake inside of her. Of course, she wanted it out, but without going under. She was scared of going under for some reason, but didn't tell them that. She made up some nonsense about being allergic." Mary paused for a minute. "As silly as it sounds, the surgeon agreed and they extracted the snake. The problem was, something went very wrong afterwards and the woman died right there on the operating table."

"So, what does that mean?" Catherine asked.

"It means, in death, she cursed this hospital and the use of that sleeping drug..."

"Anesthesia."

"Yeah. She figured the doctors didn't fight hard enough to save her life, so she claims the souls of those for Hell who least expect to die when they go under."

"But she didn't use anesthesia. Why claim the souls of people who use it?" Catherine was bewildered.

"She was afraid of it and because other people seem to be more courageous about it than she was, it's like she wants them to know fear in other ways – like what's waiting for them once they go under. It's screwed up."

"If this is true, she sounds like a malicious person who mustn't have been much different when she was alive."

"Uh huh."

"So, you said Priscilla is over there due to no fault of her own. How does her mother, Mrs. Abney, fit into this picture?"

Mary gazed at Catherine for a moment. "The child's mother was the one that caused the spell to be cast on the woman I told you about. When Priscilla got here to the hospital, the already raging spirit who has the forces of Hell awaiting those who arrive at that plane, saw it the perfect opportunity to exact revenge on the woman that caused her so much pain and who she feels ultimately, caused her her life."

"Wow. This is so weird."

"The girl came to you last night, didn't she?" Mary asked.

"It's amazing you know that," Catherine replied. "I dreamt about her."

"That was no dream, Miss Catherine. In a way it was, but in a way, it wasn't. Priscilla really needs your help. She's not going to wake up on her own. She'll remain in that coma until her body ultimately gives up. If you choose to help her, your survival in that place depends on your ability to conquer your fear. You see, it's what they feed off. It's what makes the game of cat and mouse far more interesting for them. You'd have to be extremely brave, lady. Otherwise, you won't be able to help the child because you won't survive either."

Catherine needed time to process everything, but she didn't have to think about whether or not she would help Priscilla.

"As crazy as this whole thing sounds, I believe you," Catherine said. "Priscilla must've sent you here. What do I have to do?"

Nine

11:31 a.m.

"Are you sure about this?" Mae asked.

Lying on a stretcher in an unused room on the fourth floor of the hospital, Catherine nodded. "Yes. I have to do this."

"I must be out of my mind, Catherine, because if this blows up in my face I'm out of a job and probably facing criminal charges."

Catherine took her hand. "I know you're risking everything right now to save little Priscilla. So am I, but none of this is her fault. If anything goes wrong... say, if I never wake up, I want you to deny ever knowing anything about this. This is my decision, Mae. You're not guilty of anything either way. I want your conscience to be clear, okay?"

Mae nodded apprehensively. "Okay. You're right: We're doing this for the child. She shouldn't have to waste away in a coma."

"That's my girl. Give me a minute to collect myself, then do it," Catherine said.

She closed her eyes and pictured Priscilla waiting for her. Wearing latex gloves, Mae injected her with the medication to render her hopelessly unconscious. Catherine inhaled and gradually felt herself drifting away.

* * *

Anxious and trying her best not to be noticed for it, Mae returned to the ER and hurried over just as a lady was being wheeled in.

"Head on collision!" An EMT worker said as Mae, along with other nurses and a doctor tended to the patient.

"Get her into the ER!" The doctor shouted. Mae now dreaded those words. Could this finely dressed lady in the prime of her life be yet another patient that dies under the curse Catherine had told her about? The thought of that possibility nauseated her.

* * *

Catherine found herself walking on the fourth floor of Merci Hospital. However, it didn't look the same and it certainly didn't "feel" the same. She knew she had crossed over to that place where Priscilla and the others had ended up.

"Priscilla!" She called out, well aware that doing so might draw unwanted attention to herself. She just wanted to find the girl, and somehow get the hell out of there. The place gave her the creeps.

The empty corridor had a slightly similar appearance to the one in her dream. However, straight ahead, she could clearly see where it ended on a curve. There was no door with a silver frame that supposedly led into someplace dark, yet inviting.

"Priscilla, where are you, honey? It's me. Nurse Catherine."

The silence was deafening, but she felt the stares of many as she walked on. Recalling Mary's advice, she fought against her own elevating fear knowing her survival depended upon it.

She heard the screech of a door and noticed one of the double ones that led into the ICU was slightly ajar.

"Priscilla, is that you?" She went over and pushed it open. Dozens of empty beds awaited her. Catherine walked in, passing each bed which strangely all had rumpled sheets on top and food trays at the foot of them. Up above her head was a woman in ripped, black clothing clutching onto the ceiling and delightfully peering down through jet black eyes.

Looking left and right, Catherine continued down to the end of the ward, then took a left turn to the restrooms. Upon entering, she heard a slight chuckle and her heart froze. Common sense dictated it was not Priscilla, but something sinister. She could feel the lump in her throat as she swallowed and an ominous sensation blanketed her.

With trembling fingers, she pushed open each cubicle. And the few that were locked from the inside, she stooped down to see if Priscilla was hiding in any.

"Nurse Catherine..."

Catherine swung around. The call had come from outside of the restroom. It sounded like... Priscilla.

"Honey, I'm here!" She was in the main room again. "Where are you?"

"I'm here." A deeper, raspy voice answered, then an odor permeated the room – a deathly smell Catherine knew was rotting flesh.

She ran out of the ICU and back into the corridor. By then and unbeknownst to her, the ceiling was filled with crawling ghouls, some with heavy drizzle sliding from their mouths and splattering onto the floor beneath. A few were headless, but moved around as if they had invisible eyes somewhere. Their laughter soaked up the air like water in a sponge.

Catherine clutched at her throat after reaching the hallway. She bent over and tried to catch her breath after feeling like she had literally been strangled by a force she couldn't see.

Then in her peripheral vision, she could have sworn she saw something move. Something little and something fast.

Looking over to her right, there was another door which led to a room she was not familiar with. She turned the handle and looked inside. It was a narrow closet where scores of long, white physician coats hung. *Strange*, she thought.

"Priscilla... are you in here?"

Immediately, Catherine felt a strong grip of her legs. It was Priscilla. She had crawled from under some of the coats.

Catherine picked her up and hugged her tightly. "Oh! I'm so glad you're all right!"

The child was sobbing.

Catherine wiped her tears with her fingers. "Don't cry. I'm here now. You don't have to be afraid anymore." Nevertheless, she couldn't deny she wasn't feeling her bravest.

"They can't come in here," the child whispered.

"Why not?"

"The woman in the raggedy clothes thinks these are actually doctors." She pointed to the coats. "That's what the nice lady told me."

"What woman in raggedy clothes?"

"You didn't see her?" Priscilla was surprised. Catherine shook her head. "She crawls around the walls and ceiling out there and she scares me a lot."

Catherine thought she knew who this woman might be.

"Who is the other woman you referred to – the nice lady?"

"She kept telling me to find the yellow door, but before she hid me in here, I couldn't find it anywhere. She said it's the only way out."

"Okay." Catherine rubbed the child's arm. "We're gonna find that yellow door and we're getting out of here, so you can be with your mommy again, all right."

"I miss my mommy. I kept calling for her and she couldn't hear me. That's when I called for you. The nice lady told me you would be able to hear me and you'd come. And she was right." Her eyes brimmed with tears.

Catherine stooped down next to her. "I need you to do something for me, okay, honey?"

"Uh huh."

"We're going out there together and I need you to be very strong, not just for me, but for your mommy because she really wants you to come back, okay?

Priscilla nodded.

"Whatever you see out there that might look bad, don't focus on it. Instead, focus on your mommy – on getting back to her. Those things that frightened you feed off your fear and mine. We have to show them that we're not afraid and then we'll be able to find that door faster, okay? Is it a deal?"

"Yes," Priscilla answered softly, wiping her cheeks with the back of her hands.

"Good girl. Let's go."

Ten

Catherine held Priscilla's hand as they exited the closet and walked the main corridor. They glanced at each door along the way to see if it was the one the mysterious woman had told Priscilla to find.

They made it down to the business offices. Each part of the building evoked the same uncanny sensations as both Catherine and Priscilla felt the intensity of malicious stares.

Catherine felt drawn to one of the offices. It happened to be Franklyn Radford's, as his name was neatly engraved in metal and attached to the door.

She proceeded inside the room and they immediately heard what sounded like urine trickling inside a toilet. Catherine's heart started to pound and so did Priscilla's. She gripped the child's hand even more tightly, looking down at her with a silent message to be brave.

Catherine turned the handle of the bathroom as the trickling sound continued. As the door flashed open, they saw a straggly-haired woman with black eyes and brownish, discolored teeth stooped up on the toilet. Her black, mostly shredded gown had been tossed to the side.

Priscilla screamed and Catherine slammed the door shut. They could hear the woman's hearty laughter vibrating in the walls.

They ran out of the room and down toward the exit straight ahead. "That's her!" Priscilla screamed as they ran. "She crawls all over the walls and the ceiling."

"We're okay. We're okay," Catherine replied, heading toward the exit, never easing her grip of the child's little hand. She pressed the bar that was waist high and pushed outwards, wanting nothing more than out of that building. Perhaps, this was the route even though there was nothing yellow about that door.

The exit, strangely, led into another room that appeared to be a conference room. A long, oval desk sat squarely in the middle and about a dozen leather chairs surrounded it.

Standing a few feet in, near the doorway, Catherine and Priscilla watched as five men came into view. Catherine instantly recognized two of them – Dr. Radford and the Director of Merci Hospital, Luke Bazard. They were all sitting at the table and speaking quietly.

Curious as to what it was all about, Catherine advanced closer, much to Priscilla's reluctance. She knew what she was witnessing was some time in the past and that the men could not see them.

"We had no choice," Radford said. "She was going to squeal. We had to take care of her."

"What's done is done. Not a word of this will be spoken again," Bazard said, seemingly with the weight of the world on his shoulders.

Just then, a woman appeared in the room. She was around five feet, six inches tall and of a slender build. She wore a blue nurse's uniform and had a hole in the center of her forehead. Priscilla held on to Catherine even more tightly, who immediately knew that the woman was the topic of their conversation. One or more of them had murdered her – a fellow nurse.

"She's the one who hid me and told me to find the yellow door. But she didn't have that hole in her head before," Priscilla whispered.

The woman, who had been looking down at Radford soon looked up and made eye contact with Catherine. Led to promptly close her eyes, Catherine was shown the scene as it occurred in the operating room when the snake was extracted from the "crawling woman's" abdomen. She watched as the nurse protested to the inhumane practice of the doctors in the room and how Radford killed her when she threatened to squeal. She saw how Bazard became aware after the fact, but protected the rogue doctor, mainly in order to preserve the hospital's good name.

The nurse nodded slowly as Catherine opened her eyes again. Catherine noticed that the men had disappeared and only the three of them were standing there.

"Catherine..." the woman started. "I don't want justice. I don't deserve it as I participated in the gruesome procedure as did all the others. I just need you to find the yellow door in order to close this portal for good. It was anger and malice that opened it, but love and forgiveness will seal it forever."

"Where is this door?" Catherine asked.

"Look inside of you. If all who passed through here had looked inside, they would have been given a second chance. But their consciences couldn't allow them to see clearly and so, death came for them. None before you were able to see me, although they heard me. Because they couldn't see me, I couldn't communicate this way. The evil surrounding them had become their primary focus, so they couldn't see what little good was here with them."

Catherine closed her eyes again and she could see the entire interior of the hospital. Everywhere still appeared overcast, but in one section of the building was a light that shone briskly through a glass door. She opened her eyes. "My God, the yellow door is not the color of the door itself, it's the color of the sun shining through it!"

The nurse nodded with a smile.

"Thank you," Catherine said.

She looked at Priscilla whose eyes were lit up with excitement.

"You know where it is?" The girl asked.

Catherine had a cheerful glow. "I know. Let's go home!"

They ran through a series of corridors, down two flights of stairs and into the huge space that Catherine knew to be the Neonatal Intensive Care Unit. When they walked in, Priscilla screamed and dashed behind Catherine holding tightly to her waist. The floor was covered with black, crawling insects: spiders – some jumping ones, scorpions, beetles, and scattered throughout was a variety of snakes – rattlers, cobras, pythons. Sliding along the walls were the hellish ghouls and beasts. The woman in black twisted her neck from side to side with an agitated look on her grotesque face. When Catherine saw her, she knew the woman was worried that soon all the venomous hatred and revenge might be over.

Catherine bent down and looked Priscilla in the eyes. "Remember what I told you before we left the closet? How you have to be very brave for yourself and for your mommy?"

Priscilla nodded, fighting to restrain her willful tears.

"Now, more than ever, you have to be strong. These things you see can't hurt you if you don't feed into them with fear. Although it is frightening, your love for your mommy and your mommy's love for you is more powerful. Okay?"

"Okay," Priscilla replied; her voice breaking. "I'll be strong. Will you be strong too?"

"Yes." Catherine said. "We'll both be strong. The door is straight ahead at the back. Do you see it?"

"Yes. I see the sun shining through."

"Good. As you walk, focus straight ahead on the door. Not what's going on to your left or right, nor what's happening underneath. As you step on these sickening things and hear the crunch beneath your feet, that's how much evil you are defeating and how many lives you'll be saving that will pass through these hospital doors. This hellish place will no longer exist and won't claim anymore souls. And the crawling woman and the horrible beasts around these walls will go straight to hell."

"Okay."

"Are you ready?"

"Yes." Priscilla mustered up some grit.

Catherine took her hand again and as they started walking toward the glass door which was about sixty feet away, they kept their eyes focused straight ahead.

Priscilla detested the feel under her little feet as she walked on top of the creatures, but remembered what Catherine said each step signified. The closer they got to the door, the faster the beasts encircled the walls. Catherine sensed they were the ones who feared their inevitable defeat as she and Priscilla's bold determination to live crushed them.

The walk felt like the longest one they had ever taken, and now they were close – really close. When they finally arrived, Catherine pushed open the door and a burst of sunlight lit up the entire building. All color instantly returned and Catherine woke up in the little room where Mae had reluctantly put her under.

She sat up on the stretcher with the widest smile, feeling a huge sense of relief. Getting up, she smoothed her ponytail with her hands and took the elevator a few flights down. When the doors parted, she spotted Mae standing alone at the water cooler; her hand shaking as she placed the paper cup to her mouth. Catherine wondered if anyone else had noticed the obvious – that Mae was a complete wreck.

"I'm back!" She said, with arms open wide.

Shocked by the very sight of her, Mae grabbed her and held her tightly.

"Oh, my gosh! You're back!" She exclaimed. "I was up and down the elevator checking on you to see if you were still alive. I was afraid you'd never come back!"

"Thankfully, I did." Catherine smiled.

"So how did it go? What about the little girl?"

"Come."

Catherine and Mae walked down the corridor to Priscilla's room. They saw Priscilla sitting up in bed talking with her mother. She beamed with joy when Catherine walked in and hopped off the bed and hugged her tightly.

"I was just telling mommy all about it!" Priscilla exclaimed. "How you came and saved me, the bugs and snakes and the horrible people crawling on the walls."

Tonya Abney looked up at Catherine. "I don't know where she got this story from. Sounds like she's had more of an adventure while in that coma." She laughed. "Anyway, I'm so happy that she's awake now." She hugged her daughter again. Mae was standing there, overjoyed.

"I'm happy too." Catherine said. "I'm sure they'll be discharging Priscilla soon. I want you both to know that I'm very sorry about everything that happened, but all is well that ends well, right?"

"Right," Tonya agreed.

"Priscilla, take care now." Catherine winked.

"Bye, Nurse Catherine. And thank you for saving me!"

After Catherine and Mae left the room, they heard Priscilla calling Catherine from the doorway.

"Yes, honey?"

"You forgot to give me my bag of goodies, like you promised!" Priscilla said.

Catherine giggled. "You're right! I'll be right back with them."

Mae laughed as Catherine hurried off to retrieve them.

* * *

Catherine learned that afternoon that her best friend, Amy, had been the victim of a terrible car crash. She had been admitted to Merci for emergency surgery a little before noon that day – around the time Catherine had promised to call her about meeting for lunch. It was said that once sedated, Amy never woke up. Catherine had no idea that while she was rescuing Priscilla from the portal, her dear friend might have been there at the same time.

She would never know what came of her.

Eleven

After prompting an investigation of Dr. Radford in the disappearance of thirty-eight-year-old nurse Sandra Newry, Catherine was relieved when Dr. Radford was finally arrested for her murder. A year after Sandra went missing after work, her remains were found in a shallow grave on the hospital's grounds approximately a thousand feet from the main building. Luke Bazard and three other doctors were implicated in the cover-up and faced multiple charges in that respect. All of them lost their jobs.

The unexplained deaths ceased at Merci Hospital and though its reputation had now been marred, it never stopped serving the good people of the county.

Catherine Lucene still works at Merci.

CORNELIUS

"The very first instance of a haunted house story making me cry."

Prologue

It was a day and age much like today where every town, generation and household held firmly its secrets—torrid improprieties they would protect to the end of the world. Yet some secrets back then were far too shocking and disturbing to contain— ones entangled with emotions of such intensity that would shock the very life out of 'innocent', reserved folk.

The year was 1861. The town of Mizpah was on the verge of the abolition of slavery. White people with a conscience and black folk alike prayed and fought long and hard for the day when all human beings were considered equal in the eyes of the law.

Cornelius Ferguson, only the wealthiest planter in all of Mizpah, didn't support the views of the abolitionist movement in that territory nor in any other for that matter. Negro labor was highly favorable for his pockets and he couldn't imagine conducting his plantation affairs by any other means.

June 12th of 1861 was the day his life would forever change. It was the day a colored girl by the name of Karlen Key walked through his door. She was beautiful, literate, well-spoken — a rare breed and long-awaited trade off from another planter across the river. Cornelius had been anticipating her arrival. Germina, a rotund, elderly house slave with a few long strands protruding from her chin, met Karlen at the door and showed her where to put her tattered bag. Cornelius stood thirty feet away in the great room facing the entrance way, highly pleased and mesmerized by the new addition to his household. Karlen's eyes met his for a brief moment before she quickly hung her head down, made a slight bow and greeted her master. The twenty-one-year-old had no idea that her arrival at the Ferguson plantation would alter the course of her life and those around her in a most uncanny way.

1

Summer of 1965

"Wade! Mira!" Sara Cullen called her kids from outside the kitchen door. "Time to come inside and get yourselves cleaned up for dinner!"

Fourteen-year-old, Wade and thirteen-year-old, Mira were in the road playing 'bat and ball' in front of their yard with Monique Constantakis and her cousin Philip. Mira had just swung the bat for her turn to run the bases.

"Let's go!" Wade shouted to his sister as she considered one last run before heading inside. "If you don't come now, I'm leaving you and you'll be in big trouble with Dad." On that, he took off up to the driveway of their home and Mira, with a tinge of disappointment, handed the bedraggled, semi-splintered bat to Monique who was standing behind her.

"See you later," Monique said, visibly disappointed that her new friend had to leave.

"Yeah," Mira said before heading up the driveway behind her brother who had disappeared into the house.

The table, as usual, had been beautifully set for dinner. Sara Cullen was a true perfectionist and wanted everything to be just right when her husband of fifteen years, Michael, stepped into the dining room for his meal. She worshipped the dirt the man walked on and kept herself in the finest physical shape she could possibly manage. She was five feet, ten inches tall, and remarkably thin. Her hair was long, black and curly, and her features narrow. Michael Cullen was not the most attractive man in the world, but he carried big, broad shoulders and a six-pack most men would die for. Furthermore, he collected a handsome paycheck at the end of each week, lived in a nice neighborhood, and sported a two-year-old red Jaguar. Nevertheless, Sara—Head Nurse at Freedom Hospital—could not be accused of being with him solely for his money or his executive status at the State-run Gaming Board. They had met fresh out of high school when all they had ahead of them were nothing more than dreams and aspirations.

Mira sat at the table first though Wade had been the first to wash up.

"Wade! Where are you?!" Sara cried, as she hurried around placing the remaining items on the table. The boy showed up moments later.

"Where were you all that time?" Sara asked. "You know I like both of you to be seated before I call your dad out."

"I had to... brush my hair." Wade lowered his head slightly.

"That's a lie!" Mira blurted with a wide smile. "He had to use the toilet!"

"Liar!" Wade rebutted.

"You had to use the toilet! You had to use the toilet!" Mira sang.

"Now stop it - both of you!" Sara barked. "This is no time for games... and wipe that smile off your face Mira; I'm not playing!"

"Yes, Mother," Mira softly replied.

The children composed themselves and waited patiently for their father who emerged a few minutes later from the master bedroom.

"Kids..." Michael hailed straight-faced as he sat down.

Both children responded monotonically, "Hi, Dad."

Sara joined them moments later.

As was customary for the family, they all bowed their heads at the sound of Michael's utterance, "Let us pray" before diving into their meals.

From her chair, Mira watched as her mother talked and talked to her father while he engaged very little in the conversation. It was like that all the time and Mira was beginning to wonder why her mother even tried. What Sara saw in Michael that was so appealing and attractive totally eluded Mira. Michael was a brutally rigid man who, in his daughter's opinion, always seemed to wish he was somewhere else other than at home.

"May I be excused?" Mira asked fifteen minutes later, wanting to escape the drab, depressive atmosphere of the room.

"But you hardly touched your casserole," Sara said, noticing for the first time that her daughter had barely eaten.

"I'm not hungry."

"Are you all right, honey?" Sara asked, as Michael continued his meal supposedly unaffected.

"Yes, Mom. I just feel a bit tired and would like to lie down," Mira replied.

"You may leave," Michael said, not making eye contact.

"Well then…" Sara continued, "I'll cover your plate for you in case you get hungry before bedtime."

"Thanks Mom." Mira backed out from the table and retreated to her bedroom.

Approximately a half hour later, there was a light tap at the bedroom door. The doorknob turned slowly, then Sara walked in. "Are you all right?" She asked Mira who was curled up in bed with a Sherlock Holmes mystery.

"Sure." Mira sat up as her mother proceeded to the side of the bed.

She felt her daughter's forehead with the back of her hand. "No fever. That's good. Are you sure you're okay?" The look she gave was a combination of suspicion and concern.

"Yes. I'm really fine, Mom. I just wasn't hungry; that's all—I guess from all that running around earlier."

"I see." Sara got up. "Well, like I said... if you get hungry later, your food is right there covered in the refrigerator. Wouldn't want you going to bed empty only to wake up all gassy in the morning."

Mira smiled. Her mother reached down and kissed her on the forehead. "I love you, sweet pea."

"I love you too, Mom."

2

———————————

"You wanna go by the canal today?" Wade asked Mira at the kitchen counter. An early riser, he had been up for well over an hour, but she had just gotten out of bed.

"Dad said we can't go back there—you know that," Mira answered, cracking an egg over a bowl.

"He's not here. Mom's not here. They don't have to know," Wade replied. "We can get our fishing rods, some bait, and maybe this time, we'll actually catch something."

"I don't know… the last time we got caught out there we almost got a good whipping. Dad's hand was itching. Luckily, he let us off the hook with a warning. Off the hook… got it?"

"Look! They're both at work. We'll only be gone for a few hours and will be back long before they get here. They'll never know, so we're not risking anything." Wade was adamant.

"I don't know, Wade," Mira said, pouring a little cream into the bowl with her egg.

"Why are you so scared?" Wade asked. "We've been to the canal dozens of times and only got caught that one time when dad pulled up out of nowhere. You think he's gonna drive all the way home from work today on a sneaky suspicion that we're at the canal again and bust us for not listening? Come on, Mira!"

"Okay, okay. We can go after I've had my breakfast. I suppose you've eaten already?" Mira asked.

"Yeah. I'm cool. I'll go pack the gear."

The canal was less than a block away. It usually took the kids a mere four minute walk to get there. Mira, dressed in a yellow and white striped blouse and red shorts walked quickly behind her brother, inwardly hoping and praying that their father would not pull up and surprise them while they were on the way to the 'forbidden place'.

"We need to walk faster," Mira said, now over-taking her brother. Wade silently caught up with her and in no time, they were at their favorite spot.

The canal was the only one in their neighborhood. It extended miles out to the sea. Several gated houses with boat decks surrounded it, except for a fifty-foot open area that was partially clear due to low, sparse bushes and a padded, gravel area kept in check by occasional vehicles driving through.

Mira sat down at the edge of the canal, her feet dangling against its rocky structure. Wade got the fishing rods ready before sitting next to her. He handed Mira a rod with bait attached and threw his out into the not-so-shallow water. For a while, they just sat there looking out into the water at tiny schools of fish swimming around.

"What's on your mind?" Wade asked, still looking straight ahead.

"What do you mean?" Mira glanced at him.

"You're so quiet. What're you thinking about?"

"Nothing."

"You're the one lying now," Wade said.

"How can you say that I'm lying? Are you inside my brain, Wade Cullen?" Mira returned feistily.

"It's Mom and Dad, isn't it?"

Mira looked at him. "How do you know?"

"I know what's been going on. I can see it was getting to you. That's why you left the table yesterday, right?"

For a few moments, there was silence, then Mira finally answered: "I don't understand why Mom tries so hard to please Dad. It's not like he shows her he appreciates anything she does anyway."

"We've never known Dad to be a talkative person, Mira. He doesn't say much to us neither," Wade replied.

Again... there were a few moments of silence.

"I think his actions go beyond not being much of a talker, Wade. Dad can be so cold at times. I feel so bad for Mom when I see her trying so hard to please him all the time and he doesn't seem to be giving anything back to her. It's like she's in a relationship all by herself."

"Mom's used to Dad. They're just different people. She doesn't seem to mind when she's talking to him and it's obvious that he's not even listening. If she's not bothered by it, why should you let it bother you?"

"Because she's our mother, Wade. That's why. She deserves better than that," Mira answered.

"Better than Dad?"

"I think so."

Wade was shocked that his sister's feelings about the matter were that intense. "What are you trying to say, Mira—that Dad's not good enough for Mom? Don't you love him?"

"Sure I do. I love them both, but I can tell that Mom's not happy. She pretends that she is because she lives in this 'perfect world' that she's created in her head."

Wade's eyes were on the water again. "I think I feel something..." he said moments later. "Yes! I got a bite!" He reeled in the rod as quickly as he could while Mira's eyes beamed at the prospect of him making a good catch. By then, they were both standing and watching an average-sized snapper wiggle its streamlined body on the hook.

"Yay! We got one!" Mira exclaimed.

Wade unhooked the fish and dumped it into their mother's mini cooler.

"That's a good one," Mira said, watching the fish flop around in the cooler.

"Yeah. Let's see if we can catch anymore."

They both sat back down and re-tossed their fishing rods after Wade baited his again.

A half hour passed and there was nothing. Wade could now sense Mira's restlessness. "You wanna wait a little while longer to see if we'll get another bite?" He asked.

"Na. Let's not push our luck," Mira said. "We got a fish. Let's go fry it."

After turning onto their street, Mira's eyes hit the large property straight ahead at the end of the corner. "You wanna go see if any dillies are on the trees? We can eat them with our fish," she said excitedly.

"The Ferguson property?" Wade asked.

"Yeah."

Since they would have to go past their house in order to get there, Wade said, "Okay. Let me take the cooler inside first."

Mira waited in the western side of the yard that was adjacent to the road. She was so relieved that the canal trip went well and was eager to season and fry the fish they had caught.

"Let's go," Wade appeared a minute later with an empty, plastic bag balled up in his hand. "Wanna race there?"

"Sure. Now!" Mira took off on her brother unexpectedly and knowing he had been duped, Wade ran with all his might to try and catch up to her. Mira had almost made it first to the edge of the Ferguson property before Wade's long legs finally caught up to her and overtook her. He was going so fast that he could barely cut his speed sufficiently before nearly slamming into the huge coconut tree directly in front of him. Mira laughed as she panted to catch her breath.

"You cheater!" Wade said after slumping under the tree.

"Don't blame me if I almost beat you here," Mira replied. "You always boast about being able to run faster than I can."

"Are you serious?!" Wade was flabbergasted. "I *can* run faster than you! Didn't I prove it again just now—even though you cheated, you little pipsqueak?!"

Mira advanced onto the large acreage and looked up at the dillies hanging temptingly from the large, outstretched tree branches of one of many trees that clustered the property. The Ferguson estate was comprised of approximately sixty acres of land which took up most of the road east to west, extending northwardly to the edge of another neighborhood. Wade and Mira had not walked even a good two acres of the land since they were old enough to 'explore'.

"This one's packed. You wanna climb?" Mira asked her brother. Wade was the official tree-climber of the pair since Mira was terrified of heights.

Wade got up off the ground holding his back like a man far beyond his years. "Okay. You know the drill," he said, handing her the bag.

As Wade climbed the tree, Mira readied the bag so that he could drop the dillies into it. In seconds, he was at arm's length from the nearest tree branch. It was laden with mostly semi-ripe dillies. "I'm gonna start dropping now!" He cried.

Mira opened the bag as widely as possible and positioned herself directly under her brother as he dropped the fruit one by one. As usual, the bag had missed a few of them and Mira was bending down picking up the ones that had fallen without bursting on impact.

"You can't run and you can't catch!" Wade laughed in the tree as he deliberately dropped some of the dillies while she was still stooping down to pick up the others.

"You're stupid for dropping them, Wade. You're really immature!" She snarled.

Deciding they had enough of them, Wade came down from the tree and snatched one of the dillies out of the bag. As he ate, he looked around at the large property and an idea struck him. "How about we explore this land? We've never gotten further than just a few feet in everytime we come here."

"This is private property, Wade. We can't just go exploring," Mira replied, thinking how *slow* her brother really was. After all, the large, lop-sided NO TRESPASSING sign sprayed in red was clearly visible on the fence.

"You're gonna let an old NO TRESPASSING sign stop you from walking through here? Have you ever seen the owners out here? Have you ever seen *anyone* out here?"

Mira was quiet.

"Right! That's because no one ever comes here. The place is abandoned. What's wrong with a couple of kids just walking through a vacant property with a bunch of tall trees and bushes on it? What can we possibly do to hurt the land?" Wade said sarcastically. "Come on, Sis. It'll be fun. We can pretend that we're real explorers or something."

Mira was hesitant whenever Wade presented ideas that could possibly get them into trouble. Then again… those types of ideas were the only ones he ever seemed to come up with. "What about the fish?"

"What about it?" Wade was puzzled.

"We have to fry it before Dad and Mom gets back home."

Wade looked at Mira in disbelief. "Why are you so darn scary, girl? How long do you think they've been gone? It's only been a few hours. Last I knew, they got off work in the evening and then there's traffic. It's barely noon yet."

"How do you know what time it is?" Mira asked. "You don't have a watch."

"I can estimate the time, Mira. Can't you, smarty pants?"

Mira shoved the bag of fruit at him. "Here then! You carry this." And she slowly headed out into the wooded area.

As they walked along a narrow trail, the children were fascinated by the size of the property. Trees of every kind imaginable seemed to inhabit it—pine, mangoes, bananas, avocadoes, plum, ginep. Wade and Mira stopped and picked what they wanted, adding them to the bag, and the apprehension Mira had initially felt about their so-called exploration had soon disappeared.

"This is great," she said sucking on a plum.

"Awesome!" Wade agreed. "I feel like we're in the jungle or something. How long do you think it'll take us to walk the whole perimeter?"

Mira looked at him incredulously. "Are you out of your mind?" Do you think I'm gonna walk this entire property? I hear the Fergusons' land is more than a few miles long."

"I didn't mean we should walk the whole thing today. I was asking how long you think it would take us if we decided to," Wade explained.

"I don't know… maybe an hour or two." Then her eyes were suddenly affixed to a large house that they never knew was there. "Hey, look there!" Mira pointed straight ahead.

"Wow! That's huge!" Wade exclaimed, almost in slow motion. With heightened curiosity, he started running toward it.

"Wait up!" Mira shouted, careful to do so in a lowered voice as she had no idea who or what might be inside. "Don't go in there without me!"

However, old and dilapidated with broken windows showcased along the whole front view, the house was breathtaking.

Wade climbed the colonial-style porch, stopping just about a foot away from the front door. The only thing is… there was no door—just a ten foot opening where there, most likely, used to be double doors.

Wade looked inside. Grimy white tiles covered the entire front area as far as he could see.

Mira climbed the porch moments later. "Do you see anything?" She asked softly, feeling a bit of apprehension gradually returning.

"No," Wade whispered. "Is anyone in here?" He called out hoping not to receive an answer.

They stood quietly, both decidedly ready to take off in an instant if they heard even a crack. They waited for a few seconds… nothing. Then Wade said, in not so much of a whisper anymore, "Let's go in."

Mira grasped his arm. He was just eleven months older than she was, but in a case like that where they were entering the *unknown*, he could have very well been ten years older and fifty pounds heavier as she knew 'come hell or high water', he would protect her.

Before stepping inside, Wade looked at her, "You mind letting up a bit? You're squeezing my arm."

"Oh sorry," Mira replied nervously.

They walked inside together—eyes darting in all directions of the spacious interior. The white paint on the wall was chipped in several places and the dusty floor had been speckled with creature droppings and smudges of dirt and mud. There was no furniture in sight—just a large, empty space. Wade and Mira walked slowly ahead and entered a room that looked like an extension of the living room, only separated by an arched wall.

"Hello…" Wade called out again.

"Is anyone here?" Mira said behind him, voice breaking at the end.

They proceeded through the large front area then entered what looked like the kitchen. There was one row of cabinets still attached to the upper northern section of the wall with a few missing doors. Some doors were slanted due to rusty, broken hinges. There were three other sections of the wall where only the imprint of cabinets remained presenting a theory to the observer that they might have been cleanly extracted at some point by thieves.

"This place is a mess," Mira uttered, still holding her brother's arm.

"Yeah. You notice that just about every door around here is missing?"

"Yeah."

"Let's go upstairs," Wade released Mira's grip. "Follow me."

"No way! You know I'm afraid of heights!" Mira whispered loudly.

"Just hold on to the rail. You'll be fine," Wade replied before heading up the long winding staircase.

Feeling that she would rather be with him than downstairs alone in the old, creepy house that resembled something from a horror flick, she took a deep breath in and decided to follow him. The ceiling of the house was extremely tall and as Mira carefully followed Wade up the stairs, she couldn't help but wonder how the owners ever managed to change a light bulb up there whenever necessary. As they climbed the staircase, the wood beneath their feet creaked and Mira had no idea how she would ever get back down.

They made it to the second landing and refusing at that point to look down over the rail, Mira trailed closely behind Wade who had entered one of the bedrooms.

"Wow! This room is huge!" Wade remarked, hurrying over to a large window on the western side of the room. "Hee, hee!" He laughed looking down at the yard. "The second floor of this house must be at least a hundred feet from the ground!"

Mira quietly advanced toward the entrance of what looked like the walk-in closet. As she looked in, something immediately caught her eye.

The floating image of a black woman was at the far end of the room. The apparition appeared relatively young with frazzled, black hair that hung tiredly just above her shoulders. Her face, rough and haggard, exuded a sadness that Mira could feel deep within her bones, and the thin, white dress the woman wore was drenched in what appeared to be blood around the mid-section where long trails of it had slid down to the end. Momentarily frozen by the sight of this woman, Mira's mouth hung open, yet no voice escaped. The woman's veiny eyes seemed to be begging, pleading... for something. Then her hand reached up toward Mira, re-enforcing what the little girl already felt was a cry for help. At that point, a blood-curdling scream escaped Mira's lungs and she darted outside of the room—Wade running behind her.

With a fear of heights that paled in comparison to what she saw in that room, before Mira knew it, she was at the bottom of the staircase and out of the house.

"What's wrong?" Wade called out to her in the yard. "Wait for me, Mira!"

She had run a good distance away from the house before even thinking of stopping.

"Tell me what's wrong!" Wade insisted after catching up to her. "I never saw you run that fast in my life."

"I know I shouldn't have listened to you, Wade. You're a jerk! We never should have come here," Mira blasted, walking hurriedly.

"What did *I* do?" Wade was confused.

"I don't wanna talk about it right now. I just wanna go home."

While darting out of the house, Wade had dropped the bag of fruits they had collected. The children walked home together without saying another word. Wade knew that he had to get to the bottom of what happened in that house; Mira was not going to fold up on him as she sometimes did. After all, he felt responsible for her and now guilty that she had been so traumatized by something that in spite of her fear of heights, she had run down a tall flight of stairs without giving it a second thought.

After arriving home, Mira went straight to her room and slammed the door. Wade went to the door and knocked lightly. "Mira... what happened back there?" He tried to turn the doorknob, but discovered it was locked. "Open up. I wanna talk to you."

"Go away!" Mira yelled.

With head hung low and feeling worse by the second, Wade asked: "What about the fish? Aren't we gonna fry it before Mom and Dad get back?"

"I don't care. Do what you want with it!" Mira replied.

"Why do you have to be like this? Why can't you just tell me what happened, Mira? You say I'm immature, but you're the immature one!"

Wade waited for a response, but didn't get one, so he went into the kitchen to prepare the fish.

After scaling and seasoning their catch, he walked around to the side of the house, made an outdoor fire like he and Mira had done so many times and placed a tin frying pan on top of the heap. As the oil heated inside the pan, Wade sat on one of the two large rocks close by, elbow under chin, thinking of how good their day had been and how it ended up. He felt terrible for Mira and wished she didn't get in those quiet moods sometimes, thus closing herself off to the world. She didn't realize that whenever she did that, he felt completely lost.

After the oil came to a slight boil, he put the fish in the pan and watched as swarms of flies suddenly appeared out of nowhere around it. Shooing them away, Wade refused to go inside and cook on the stove: He and Mira had established something special together out there frying their catch on the make-shift stove and no army of flies was going to change that.

After turning the fish over with a spatula, Wade looked up and saw Mira approaching. She went and sat down on the other large rock near the fire. Wade, elated that his sister had decided to join him, showed no reaction.

"The fish looks good," Mira said, looking at her brother.

Unable to hold back any longer, Wade asked: "What happened in that house, Mira? Why did you leave like that?"

Mira looked down for a moment. "I'm not sure. I thought… I saw something."

"Saw what?" Wade probed, curiosity in over-drive.

"I saw a woman, okay?" Mira decided to just get it out in spite of how crazy it might sound. "She was wearing a long, white dress—looked old fashioned to me—and it was covered in blood."

Wade gawked. "Are you serious?"

"'Course, I'm serious!" Mira snapped. "You think I would've took off like that for nothing?"

"Where was she?"

"In the closet."

"What was she doing?"

"Just standing there," Mira replied. "She seemed so sad. Well, I'm not going back there anymore. I don't care about dillies or anything else. I'm never going back on that property."

"I wonder why she's there." Wade was engrossed in thought.

"So you believe me?" Mira asked, feeling hopeful.

"Sure, I do. I know you'd never make something like that up. Besides, from the way you took off down those stairs, you had to see something." He laughed.

Mira smiled, then laughed out loud. Wade jumped on that opportunity to tease her as they sat and waited for their fish to cook.

BUY CORNELIUS AT AMAZON

"The very first instance of a haunted house story making me cry."

143

About The Author

Tanya R. Taylor has worn many hats throughout the years as a wife, mother, entrepreneur, and author (just to name a few). She has been writing since she could remember holding a pencil and published her first book titled: *A Killing Rage* as a young adult. She is now the author of both fiction and non-fiction literature. All of her books have already made Amazon Kindle's Top 100 Paid Best-sellers' List in several categories. Tanya writes in various genres including: Paranormal Romance, Fantasy, Thrillers, Science fiction, Mystery and Suspense.

Her book **Cornelius,** the first installment in a successful series, climbed to number one **in Amazon's Teen & Young-adult Multi-generational Family Fiction** category. And **INFESTATION: A Small Town Nightmare** is now a number one international bestseller.

Don't forget to join **Tanya's Mailing List** by signing up at **<u>www.tanyaRtaylor.com</u>**.

You'll be among the first to be notified of New Releases!

Printed in Great Britain
by Amazon

10790970R00088